NATURE IN THE NEWS

THE INDIAN OCEAN TSUNAMI

Greg Roza

PowerKiDS press.

New York

Published in 2007 by The Rosen Publishing Group, Inc.
29 East 21st Street, New York, NY 10010

Book Design: Michael J. Flynn

Photo Credits: Cover © Choo Youn-Kong/AFP/Getty Images; cover (light effect) © Taewoon
Lee/Shutterstock; interior texure background © Maja Schon/Shutterstock; p. 5 © John
Russell/AFP/Getty Images; p. 9 © Hulton Archive/Getty Images; p. 13 © STF/AFP/Getty Images;
p. 17 © Daniel Berehulak/Getty Images; pp. 19, 27 © Jewel Samad/AFP/Getty Images; p. 23 ©
Adek Berry/AFP/Getty Images; p. 25 © Paula Bronstein/Getty Images; p. 29 © Deshakalyan
Chowdhury/AFP/Getty Images.

Library of Congress Cataloging-in-Publication Data

Roza, Greg.
  The Indian ocean tsunami / Greg Roza.
       p. cm. — (Nature in the news)
  Includes index.
  ISBN-13: 978-1-4042-3538-8
  ISBN-10: 1-4042-3538-8 (library binding)
  1. Earthquakes—Juvenile literature. 2. Tsunamis—Indian Ocean—Juvenile literature. 3. Indian
Ocean Tsunami, 2004—Juvenile literature. I. Title. II. Series.
  QE521.3.R695 2006
  909'.09824083—dc22
                                                2006015698

Manufactured in the United States of America

CONTENTS

DEADLY DISASTER

On December 26, 2004, a huge earthquake shook the floor of the Indian Ocean about 150 miles (241 km) west of the Indonesian island of Sumatra. Earthquakes this big, which are known as **megathrusts**, are rare. This earthquake was the most powerful in 40 years and one of the most powerful in recorded history.

The Indian Ocean earthquake created a tsunami (soo-NAH-mee) that caused widespread damage on the island of Sumatra and other areas around the Indian Ocean. Almost 200,000 people died and another 42,000 are missing, making this natural **disaster** the deadliest tsunami in recorded history.

This photo shows people running from the first of three tsunami waves to hit Koh Raya, an island owned by Thailand. The photographer escaped to higher ground just after taking this photo.

Andaman
Islands
○ Port Blair

MYANMAR

THAILAND

Nicobar
Islands

Banda Aceh○

MALAYSIA

INDIAN
OCEAN

INDONESIA

Sumatra

5

WHAT IS AN EARTHQUAKE?

The Earth's crust or outer layer is made up of **tectonic plates**. These plates rest on the hot, soft mantle, the layer of Earth between the crust and the core or center. When the plates run into or slide over each other, the ground shakes. We call this shaking motion an earthquake.

Most earthquakes occur at a **fault line** in Earth's crust. This is an area where two plates meet. Pressure between plates causes them to bend. Finally these plates break and snap into a new position. This sudden movement is what causes an earthquake. Most larger earthquakes are followed by **aftershocks**, or smaller earthquakes.

This drawing shows some of the plates that make up Earth's crust. Each plate is about 60 miles (96.5 km) thick, and moves a few inches (cm) a year.

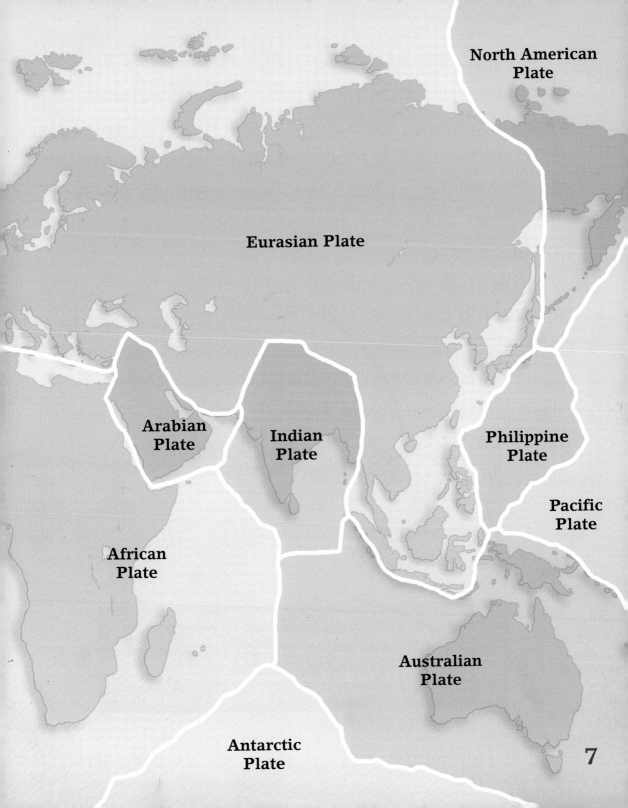

North American
Plate

Eurasian Plate

Arabian
Plate

Indian
Plate

Philippine
Plate

Pacific
Plate

African
Plate

Australian
Plate

Antarctic
Plate

7

When plates break and snap into new positions, this causes vibrations that scientists call **seismic waves**. Seismic waves move away from the **epicenter** of the earthquake in much the same way that ripples spread when you drop a pebble in a puddle of water. The further away from the epicenter, the weaker the waves become.

The shaking of the ground during an earthquake can destroy buildings and other structures on Earth's surface. Earthquakes can also change the course of rivers, create deep cracks in Earth's surface, and cause landslides. When they occur on the ocean floor, earthquakes can also cause tsunamis.

In 1906, San Francisco, California, was destroyed by an earthquake. The quake leveled about 28,000 buildings and started many fires that burned for days. Scientists learned a great deal about fault lines and seismic waves from this earthquake.

9

WHAT IS A TSUNAMI?

A tsunami is a giant wave or series of giant waves caused by an undersea earthquake, volcanic eruption, or landslide. These events can cause the surface of the ocean to swell. Tsunamis—sometimes called seismic sea waves—can be 100 feet (30 m) tall!

The speed of a tsunami depends on the depth of the water through which it passes. Out at sea, a tsunami can reach a speed of up to 600 miles (965 km) per hour. As the wave moves into shallower water near a coast, its speed drops to about 100 miles (161 km) per hour. However, the wave increases in height as it slows down, making it more dangerous.

This series of drawings illustrates how a tsunami forms. ▶

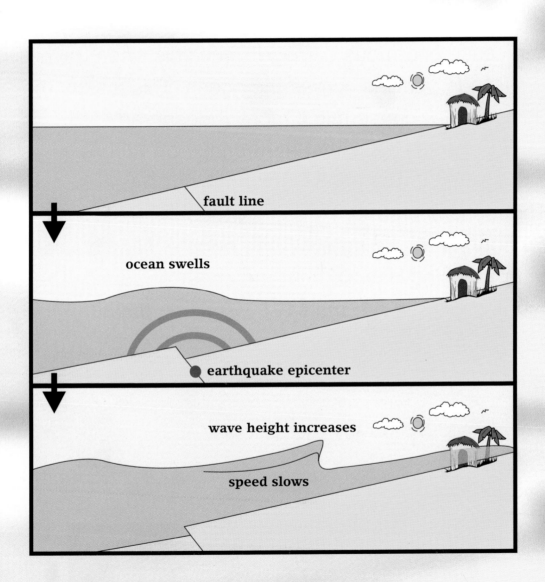

fault line

ocean swells

earthquake epicenter

wave height increases

speed slows

At sea, tsunamis can pass by unnoticed because it takes up to 30 minutes for one to pass. When a tsunami reaches land, it forms a huge wall of water that can cause enormous damage. Tsunamis often travel thousands of miles across the ocean. This makes the damage they cause much more widespread.

In 1960, the largest earthquake on record occurred off the coast of Chile, South America. The tsunami created by this earthquake hit Hawaii 14 hours later, killing sixty-one people. Nine hours after reaching Hawaii, it hit the coast of Japan. The tsunami killed more than 120 people in Japan.

The earthquake and tsunami of 1960 killed more than 2,000 people and caused $550 million in property damage. This picture shows buildings destroyed by the earthquake on Castro, an island off the coast of Chile.

13

SUMATRA AND THE ANDAMAN ISLANDS

Scientists call the Indian Ocean tsunami the Sumatra-Andaman earthquake and tsunami. This is because the fault line that **ruptured** stretches from Sumatra to the Andaman Islands.

This area of the world has a long history of seismic activity. In August 1883, a volcano south of Sumatra named Krakatau (kra-kuh-TOW) erupted. Most of the volcanic island sank into the sea, creating a powerful tsunami 130 feet (40 m) high. The wave killed 36,000 people on Sumatra, Java, and other nearby islands. Tsunamis were observed throughout the Indian and Pacific Oceans, and even as far away as the west coasts of North and South America.

> On June 26, 1941, an earthquake occurred about 62 miles (100 km) northwest of Port Blair. The quake destroyed the city of Port Blair and created a tsunami that killed nearly 5,000 people in India.

INDIA

THAILAND

**1941
epicenter**
Andaman
Islands

Port Blair •

Nicobar
Islands

SRI LANKA

Banda Aceh •

MALAYSIA

2004 epicenter

fault line

Sumatra

INDONESIA

Krakatau

Java

DECEMBER 26, 2004

The Indian Ocean earthquake occurred at 7:59 a.m. on December 26, 2004. About 808 miles (1,300 km) of underwater fault line slipped about 33 feet (10 m). One plate suddenly broke free and slipped under the other plate. This occurred in two stages over a period of several minutes. It was one of the four largest quakes on record, with a **magnitude** between 9.0 and 9.3 on the **moment magnitude scale**. The earthquake was felt as far away as India and Thailand.

The earthquake's epicenter was at the southern end of the fault rupture, about 150 miles (241 km) west of northern Sumatra. The energy released from the fault rupture was about equal to the energy of 23,000 **atomic bombs**!

The Indian Ocean earthquake was the strongest quake in 40 years and the fourth-strongest quake since scientists began measuring them in 1899.

The fault rupture that occurred during the earthquake caused the ocean floor to rise up several meters. This caused a huge **displacement** of water. The surface of the Indian Ocean swelled above the entire length of the 808-mile (1,300-km) rupture, creating tsunamis.

About 15 minutes after the quake occurred, a wall of water between 80 and 100 feet (24 and 30 m) high smashed into the western shore of Sumatra, a region named Banda Aceh (BAHN-duh AH-chee). A similar wave hit the Andaman and Nicobar Islands. The people on the beaches and shore were given no warnings to leave. They had no idea what was about to happen.

This photo of Banda Aceh, Indonesia—taken about 21 days after the earthquake occurred— clearly shows the destruction that can result from a tsunami.

The waves spread out from the epicenter to the east and the west. Most of the eastern wave hit Sumatra, but it also hit Thailand and Malaysia. The western tsunami traveled a great distance and hit other countries around the Indian Ocean, including India and Sri Lanka (SREE LAHN-kuh). The tsunami continued across the Indian Ocean and completely destroyed twenty of the 199 low-lying Maldives. The waves hit the eastern coast of Africa 7 hours after the earthquake occurred, causing the worst damage in Somalia. People living on the Pacific coast of North and South America also observed small tsunamis. Some were as large as 8.5 feet (2.6 m).

The tsunamis traveled east and west from the epicenter. This meant that areas to the north, like Bangladesh, received very little damage. ▶

Bangladesh

India

Myanmar

Thailand

Somalia

Sri Lanka

Malaysia

Kenya

Maldives

anzania

Indonesia

Seychelles

Madagascar

INDIAN
OCEAN

countries affected by the tsunami

21

DESTRUCTIVE FORCES

The areas that were hit hardest were Indonesia and the Andaman and Nicobar Islands. On the island of Sumatra, the tsunami reached close to 2 miles (3.2 km) inland, wiping the land clean of life. Some reports estimated that almost 70 percent of the population of coastal villages on Sumatra were killed by the tsunami. Nearly 131,000 Indonesians lost their lives, and more than 500,000 were left homeless. Sadly, relief agencies like the Red Cross reported that nearly one-third of the people killed by the tsunami were children.

In addition to the local people who died, thousands of vacationers lost their lives. Most of these people were from Europe.

Like many towns in the Aceh region of Sumatra, this mosque is all that remained in Meulaboh after the tsunami receded. All other structures were washed away.

Indonesia got the worst of the tsunami's power, but other countries also suffered damage and loss of life. After Indonesia, the island country of Sri Lanka suffered more deaths and damage than any other country affected by the tsunami. About 35,000 people died in Sri Lanka.

After Indonesia and Sri Lanka, the countries that experienced the most significant destruction include India (12,400 deaths), Thailand (5,400 deaths), the Maldives (82 deaths), Somalia (78 deaths), Malaysia (69 deaths), and Myanmar (61 deaths). Waves as high as 33 feet (10 m) hit the southeastern coast of Madagascar. Although there were no deaths, more than 1,000 people were left homeless.

Sri Lanka's tourism and fishing industries suffered greatly. In addition, more than 88,000 homes were destroyed or badly damaged, leaving about 500,000 people homeless. ▶

THE AFTERMATH

Many aftershocks occurred during the next 24 hours. In the months that followed the earthquake, thousands of aftershocks occurred and continued to frighten survivors.

On March 28, 2005—92 days after the initial quake—a second major earthquake occurred in the Indian Ocean. This quake had a magnitude of 8.7 on the moment magnitude scale but did not produce significant tsunamis. The second quake resulted in about 1,300 deaths. In the months following this quake, five more significant quakes were recorded in the area. Scientists debated whether or not these quakes were actually aftershocks of the 2004 quake.

Some scientists believe the 2004 earthquake caused two volcanoes on the island of Sumatra to erupt in the months following the quake. Other reports say that small mud volcanoes formed on some of the Andaman Islands.

The 2004 earthquake was so powerful that scientists reported that the seismic waves from the earthquake could still be measured a week after the quake occurred. Seismic instruments in the state of Oklahoma were able to record the vibrations more than 9,000 miles (14,481 km) away from the epicenter.

The quake and tsunami caused significant changes to Earth. It caused our planet to wobble on its **axis** and affected Earth's **rotation**. Scientists think that the quake shortened the length of a day by as much as 2.68 **microseconds**. The tsunami also changed the shape of coastlines in Indonesia.

Seismic activity caused small islands around Sumatra, as well as the Andaman and Nicobar Islands, to shift their positions significantly, perhaps as much as 4.1 feet (1.2 m). Some islands disappeared completely.

Car Nicobar Island

RELIEF FROM AROUND THE WORLD

The Indian Ocean disaster affected so many people that the governments of Indonesia and Sri Lanka were unable to properly care for the survivors. Relief agencies around the world sent volunteers, food and water, medicine, building materials, and money to help the survivors. Without the aid of relief agencies, many more survivors would have died from injuries, diseases, hunger, and other problems.

Despite the horrible consequences, people have learned from this disaster. Scientists are developing response plans to help reduce the harmful effects of tsunamis. They are also trying to perfect an early warning system to help alert people when a tsunami is approching.

GLOSSARY

aftershock (AF-tuhr-shahk) A smaller earthquake that often follows a larger one.

atomic bomb (uh-TAH-mihk BAHM) A bomb whose power is due to the sudden release of energy resulting from the splitting of an atom.

axis (AK-suhs) An imaginary line through Earth from top to bottom. Earth spins around its axis.

disaster (dih-ZAS-tuhr) An event that causes widespread damage, death, and hardship.

displacement (dihs-PLAY-smuhnt) The moving of something from its usual location.

epicenter (EH-pih-sehn-tuhr) The exact location on Earth's surface directly above the spot where an earthquake starts.

fault line (FAWLT LYN) A crack in Earth's crust.

magnitude (MAG-nuh-tood) A measure of the energy of an earthquake.

megathrust (MEH-guh-thruhst) A very large, rare earthquake caused when one tectonic plate "slips" under another.

microsecond (MY-kroh-seh-kuhnd) One millionth of a second.

moment magnitude scale (MOH-muhnt MAG-nuh-tood SKAYL) A scale used to measure the energy released by an earthquake. It was introduced in 1979 and is used instead of the Richter scale for very large earthquakes.

rotation (roh-TAY-shun) A turning motion.

rupture (RUHP-shur) To break suddenly.

seismic wave (SYZ-mihk WAYV) A wave caused by an earthquake that travels through Earth.

tectonic plate (tehk-TAH-nihk PLAYT) One of the many sections of Earth's crust that float on a layer of hot, soft rock.